SNOW PRINCE

TO SAVE A PONY

SALLY MARSH

Snow Prince – To Save a Pony

Formatted by Frostbite Publishing

This book is dedicated to my daughter Gemma and her best friend Katie who inspire me every day with their determination, dedication and passion.
"Keep cantering girls!"

SPECIAL THANKS

Front cover star is 'Cregduff Diamond', a Class 1 Connemara stallion belonging to Holly Norman.

Huge thanks to Holly for allowing me to use him as 'Snow Prince'.

WHAT WOULD YOU DO IF THE HORSE
OF YOUR DREAMS FELL AT YOUR FEET...?

PROLOGUE

*S*itting on her Grandmother's dapple grey rocking horse, the young girl closes her eyes and as she gently rocks it back and forth she begins to imagine that he is real. In her mind they are galloping up a far away hill towards a fire-like sunset which will take them on wonderful adventures. As they go faster and faster she winds her delicate fingers around his long mane and grips tight. The top of the hill is approaching and still her horse gallops on, his hooves making no sound as they hit the dusty ground again and again...

Suddenly a voice stirs her from her trance and in an instant the dream ends as she is lifted from her steed.

"Time for bed" her grandmother whispers, "maybe one day that horse will come to life..."

*T*earing her bedroom curtains open to reveal a frosty Autumn morning, Jenna Waters shuddered at the thought of heading out to catch the school bus. But with the thought that it was her last day before the half term break she spun on her bare heels, threw her pink fluffy dressing gown on and skipped down the wooden stairs for breakfast.

The reason she was in a particularly good mood was that in two days time the whole family would be starting a new life in the countryside. It wasn't just any old new house in the countryside it was a cottage that had its own piece of land and a small wood attached to it. Jenna had already driven her parents crazy with the constant questions about the cottage and the area it was in and if there were riding stables nearby. She had always been animal mad but horses and ponies were her passion.

Jenna's bedroom walls were typically covered in inspiring images torn from the endless pony related magazines she bought with her pocket money and her shelves and windowsill were laden with model horses of every size and colour. Jenna's passion had been sparked when on her 13th birthday her parents had bought her a set of 6 riding lessons at the local riding stables located on the out skirts of the city. She could still remember every smell and sound from the first moment she had stepped out of her parents car and onto the yard on the day of the first lesson, it had been like something out of a movie. The smell of fresh hay and sweaty ponies mingled with the sound of echoing hooves and laughing voices, Jenna had felt like she belonged there instantly! Everything had come so naturally to her with the riding and her instructor Ingrid had said so to her parents much to Jenna's delight. At the end of the 6 lessons Jenna was cantering around the sand arena aboard Jet the steady black fell pony who she always rode. He was calm and steady with a mane so long it would flow past her knees as she trotted round the arena and she would brush his mane for hours until it was knot free and silky.

When the lessons finished Jenna had earned her lessons by mucking out the stables and cleaning the endless pile of riding tack, not that she minded as the smell of leather was nearly as good as the smell of the ponies when she buried her face in their soft necks.

Ingrid lived not far from the family home and would pick Jenna up on her way to the stables, on the journey there they would chat about the funny things the ponies got up to and the latest news from the biggest shows. Ingrid had done a lot of show jumping in the past until a nasty fall in which she broke her shoulder badly had caused her to retire early. Her best horse had been called Storm Chaser and he still lived at the yard with Ingrid and was occasionally used for lessons if one of the other horses was out of action. Jenna had always wanted to ride him but the opportunity had not arisen and she was not brave enough to ask Ingrid if she could even just sit on him. This weekend would be the last at Kingston farm for Jenna and every time she thought about it a lump would rise in her throat and she wondered where she would get her 'pony fix' when they got to the new house? Her parents had assured her that there were plenty of riding stables in the area and she sure hoped they were right!

As she sat down at the breakfast bar in the kitchen her mum Karen came through the back door with the family's scruffy little terrier Betsy under her arm, the little dog wriggled and squeaked as it spotted Jenna and wagged its stumpy tail in affection before Karen put her down on the floor. Betsy immediately rushed over to Jenna and bounced up and down at her bare legs desperate for a fuss which was exactly what she got. "Make sure you wash your hands before you touch any food" tutted Karen "That dog has been trying to dig through to the neighbours again," this made Jenna giggle as she swung her legs off the stool and went to the sink to wash her hands. Spotting the clock on the wall was now showing 7.50am Jenna decided she had better get some breakfast fast, she grabbed the bread from the side and dropped it in the toaster. She used the toaster to time how quickly she could get dressed and raced back up the stairs nearly flattening her brother Ed as she went, luckily he was used to this routine and side-stepped her like a pro as she hurtled past. Ed was 15 only 2 years older than Jenna but they were totally different people, he lived for computers and cars and always had his head in the latest magazines. Jenna was of course animal mad but also very headstrong and always knew what she wanted and worked hard to get it. Tights on, skirt on, polo shirt on and cardigan half on as she tore back down the stairs in record time nearly tripping over Betsy as she headed for the toaster only to discover that Ed had raided it and was heading off out the door with the toast in his mouth! "Noooooooooo Ed, that was mine!" screeched Jenna but it was too late Ed was off down the path and gone. " He is so annoying mum, why does he have to do that?" complained Jenna but her mum just chuckled and replied "Because he's your brother!"

On the bus ride to school Jenna sat next to the window, her head resting against the cold damp glass as she watched the streets flash past. People scuttled along with hoods pulled up tight against the lashing rain, the occasional bedraggled dog trotting at their heels. She always felt sorry for the dogs, not the owners. One day she dreamed she would own her own rescue shelter and fill it with unfortunate animals who needed her help or rescuing from bad people. Before her mind could drift anymore the bus pulled into the school layby and its occupants bundled to the doors to be the first off. Jenna could never understand why and always sat and waited for the scrum to die down, she wanted to savour every bit of today especially as it was her last. Although she didn't hate school she didn't really enjoy it much either. She was yet to meet anyone as animal mad as she was and despite having a couple of good friends who she would miss she was hopeful that her new school being countryside based would offer up a real friend who would want to race around the fields on prancing ponies or rescue kittens from abandoned barns. Only time would tell and this weekend amongst the madness of packing boxes she would have to bid her beloved Kingston Farm goodbye and start the 4 hour journey to her new home that she had not even seen yet.

Jenna had been away at a school summer camp when her Dad had got the job offer so everyone but she had been to see the cottage. Everything had happened so fast life during the last couple of months had been a whirlwind of changes and chaos. The last day at school went surprisingly quickly with all her class mates and teachers being very sweet and she had been given good luck cards and enough chocolate to last her a month. Jade and

Chloe her two closest friends at the school had promised to visit in a few weeks when Jenna and the rest of the family had settled properly and she hoped that they would keep their promises.

Arriving back home to a house stacked with boxes of all shapes and sizes Jenna squeezed her way through the packed hall way and went straight to the fridge for a cold drink. Her dad had already done two trips to the new place with a heap of boxes but on Monday a removals firm would be arriving to pack up the rest of their things and take them to their new life in the Yorkshire countryside. All Jenna could think about really was that the area was famous for its rolling hills and breathtaking views, Ideal for riding! What adventures awaited her? She couldn't wait to find out, Monday couldn't come soon enough!

*T*he clattering of something tumbling down the stairs and landing with a thump was what woke Jenna sharply from her blissful sleep. She sat up tutting as she struggled to sweep her long wayward hair from over her face. Swinging her legs out of bed she stumbled to the bedroom door and peered out. From downstairs she could hear busy voices and her mum was asking for someone to bring her a dust-pan and brush because she had managed to knock one of the potted plants off the windowsill while coming down the stairs laden with boxes. Jenna retreated back into her room and sat on her bed. Today was the day, it was moving day! She sprang up went to her wardrobe and pulled on leggings and a loose fitting top, scraped her hair into a quick pony tail, then skipped off down the stairs treading on bits of plant and soil as she went!

Downstairs it was mayhem! Two strange men in yellow overalls were ferrying boxes out to a big yellow and white lorry parked right out side the house, Jenna's mum called her name and she headed for the kitchen."Come on you!" scolded her mum, "No time for a lie in today, we've got too much to do and we are already behind schedule". She handed Jenna a huge box and jammed some cold toast between her teeth before Jenna could complain and pointed in the direction of the lorry. Finally after another 2 hours of loading the lorry and both the cars they were ready to leave. Standing in the empty, now cold living room Jenna felt a sad feeling creep over her and she shuddered slightly at the thought of the big change about to happen. Too late now though, the decision was made and exciting adventures lay ahead for the whole family. "Come on Jenna, time to go" whispered her dad as he put a warm, strong arm around her shoulder and guided her to the box laden car.

That was it, they were off! Some of their neighbours had come out to wave them off and after a lot of waving and shouts of good luck the cars and lorry slowly pulled out and headed off on the long journey to the family's new life. Jenna pulled out her iPod, placed the headphones in her ears and as the music softly played she gazed out of the window, watching as the grey city buildings turned slowly into park lands and then into open countryside. To pass the time she played a game with herself by trying to spot different coloured horses as the car passed their fields. Jenna's favourite colour was dapple grey as it reminded her of the beautiful rocking horse that her grandmother had in her attic. Jenna had spent hours as a young child sitting on its back and imagining cantering through fields and woodlands to rescue her friends from mudslides and bad people. Its mane had been made from real horse hair and was so long it almost touched the floor, it had a proper handmade leather saddle and bridle and large black eyes that looked like any minute they would blink. The rocking horse had been called Cloud Dancer and his name had conjured up so many stories for Jenna's Grandmother to tell her at night, Jenna would close her eyes and imagine every tiny detail as if she were really there. It had always been her dream to own a real life horse that looked like Cloud Dancer and as her eyes scanned the countryside she wondered if that dream would ever come true.

"How long until we get there?" Jenna asked as she removed her headphones and leaned forward. She stretched her arms up above her head and yawned whilst she awaited her dad's response. "Well" replied her dad catching Jenna's eye in the rear view mirror, "I reckon in half an hour we will be there, as long as there are no hold ups" he grinned. "OK that's cool" she sighed as she slunk back into her seat and began scanning the fields again for anything pony shaped. Ahead of them a large grey stone farmhouse came into view, it looked pretty rundown with broken fencing and old machinery littering the fields surrounding it. As they got closer Jenna kept her fingers crossed that no unfortunate animals were kept in such mayhem but as they got level with the farm she spotted a black and white collie chained to a ramshackle kennel. The poor thing looked so sad and unloved that Jenna nearly yelled at her dad to stop the car but her attention was suddenly taken by the silhouette of a horse trotting across one of the road-side fields. With the pale winter sun in her eyes she struggled to get a good look but as they got level with the horse her dad slowed the car down as he came up behind a cyclist. Jenna could see that a man was out in the same field with an armful of hay which he started to hold out to the horse which had steadied to a walk with its neck out stretched to grab the food. The horse was around 14 hands high and through the thick mud that covered its fine frame she could see it was a dapple grey. Its forelock was so long it almost touched its nostrils and Jenna heard herself whisper 'Cloud Dancer. In a flash the man with the hay suddenly produced a long looped rope and threw it neatly over the horses out stretched neck and pulled tight. The grey horse immediately panicked rearing high and leaping at the scruffy man who had on thinking the horse would run backwards fully braced himself and was leaning back, resulting in him toppling backwards into the mud and releasing his grip on the rope.

The horse with pure panic in its eyes bolted along the fence line with the rope tangling round its legs sending it into a flat out gallop. Jenna's heart started to beat faster and she knew what was about to happen. " Dad, stop the car" she yelled and the panic in her voice made him slam on the brakes just in time as the grey horse blindly galloped towards the thick hedge which surrounded the field and in a scrabbling leap it crashed through the top of the hedge and landed neatly on the road. Everything seemed to happen in slow terrifying motion and as the animal landed its legs became tangled in the trailing rope which had also become trapped in the hedge. This resulted in the rope pulling tight flipping the horse onto its side in the middle of the road.

With the terrified horse thrashing in the road Jenna ripped her seat belt off and leapt from the car. Her parents followed closely behind shouting at her to keep back as the horse lay kicking and gasping for breath as the rough rope tightened round its throat. "We've got to get him free" Jenna screeched as she reached the stricken horse. "Jenna keep back please" pleaded her mum as Jenna neared the grey's side. The horses breathing was making a rasping noise which she knew was a bad sign. "Steady boy, Steady" Jenna whispered her trembling hand outstretched as she reached his mud crusted neck. As her hand met and touched his neck the horse jolted then lay still, an awful wheezing sound coming from its flared nostrils. "He can't breathe, he can't breathe" she hissed to her parents as they got to her side. "We've got to get the rope off now!" she pleaded but as her shaking fingers felt the rope she discovered to her horror that the rope was pulled so tight the was no possible way to release it. "We need a knife to cut the rope" Jenna shouted to her parents, her voice cracking as she held her fear in. "Quickly!"

Her dad fumbling in his jacket pocket swiftly produced a small red handled pen knife which Jenna grabbed and opened in a flash. The blade was small and blunt but with a bit of effort she managed to cut through the rough rope and within a few seconds the horse was free.

He still lay slumped in the road and Jenna managed to slip her fingers between the rope and the horses throat releasing the pressure and as air flowed into his lungs again the gelding coughed and struggled to a sitting position. "It's OK boy, you're OK just stay there" She whispered as her own trembling hand stroked his gentle face. The horse lowered his head slightly and pushed into Jenna's touch as if he knew she was helping. Feeling a rush of love Jenna turned to call to her parents that the horse was OK but before she could open her mouth something stopped her. "Get off my horse now!"

came a sharp voice from behind her and before Jenna could answer the scruffy man she had seen trying to catch the horse appeared behind her. " He might be injured" she pleaded as the scruffy man grabbed the remaining rope that hung round the horses neck and swiftly threw another halter onto the horse's head. Yanking the horse to its shaking feet the scruffy man dragged the horse back towards the farm entrance. The gelding tried to neigh but all that came out was a rasping gasp.

Jenna stood rooted to the spot, how could anyone be so cruel? She just couldn't believe what had just happened. Without even a thank you the scruffy man and the poor horse melted back into the farm and out of sight.

Her Mum's warm arm guided a trembling Jenna back to the car and the family continued on their journey in silence. As they passed the rest of the farm she spun round in her seat to catch a last glimpse of the horse but there was no sign and as they headed down the hill she broke the silence in the car, "Dad we need to go back" yelled Jenna, "Jenna what on earth are you on about?" scoffed her Dad "If you think I'm turning this car around after seeing what that farmer was capable of you must be joking!". "But Dad the horse.." Started

Jenna but her dad cut her off "There is nothing we can do for that horse I'm afraid love," " What you did was brave but stupid and you could have been injured." Jenna started to protest again but her dad simply caught her eyes again in the mirror and said "No".

3

*S*till sulking, Jenna remained silent for the rest of the journey her arms folded tightly across her chest while hot tears made shiny trails down her pale face. Her mind had not stopped whirling with images of the grey horse and she wondered if he was injured and what would happen to him now. She had spent such a short time with him but her thoughts were filled images of him shivering in a field while icy rain trickled down his long wavy, matted mane Why was the scruffy man so heartless towards him? She had felt such a powerful emotion as she stroked his muddy face that she couldn't forget what had happened. Before she could think any more the car slowed down and turned left down a short gravel track that was pitted with waterfilled holes. As the car bumped along it her mum spun round in her seat with a huge grin on her face and said "We're here!" "Isn't it exciting Jenna? "Look there are fields all around and even a woodland at the bottom of the back paddock!" "Back Paddock? "Those words snapped Jenna out of her glum trance,she sat bolt up right and ripped her earphones out, had she heard right? "Did you say back paddock?" her Mum laughed and nodded " we thought it might be a nice surprise for you".

As the car pulled up outside the red bricked house Jenna leapt out and stood gazing at the at the battered sign that was screwed to the wall, sweeping away the dead ivy that covered most of it revealed the name "High Forest Farm". Jenna couldn't believe her eyes, a farm? They were going to be living on a farm?Oi!Her Brother yelled "Come on you, help with the boxes" "Just leave her for a bit" scolded Jenna's Mum, "she hasn't been here before like we have" "Go on Jenna, you can explore, I know you will want to check out all the facilities outside before you choose a bed room" she laughed. Jenna needed no second offer and excitedly pushed open the wooden gate at the side of the house and ran the short distance to the edge of the paddock that was directly behind the house. She couldn't take it all in and just didn't know where to look first, surely this was a dream? She pinched her now trembling arm hard "Ouch!" no it definitely was real, she was moving into a farm!

The damp Autumn air made her shiver even more but she wrapped her arms round her body and carried on towards to paddock. The ramshackle post and rail fencing needed a lot of repair but Jenna was already picturing what it would look like all smart and new. She pushed open the gate but it dropped off its hinges and dug into the ground. Squeezing through the gap, she turned and looked back towards the house, its red brick walls really stood out against the white framed windows making it look like the classic farmhouses Jenna had often seen in various magazines.

Turning back towards the paddock and the woodland beyond she started to walk purposefully , ready to explore but her plans were scuppered as her brothers voice broke the silence. "Jenna, Mum says you have to come and choose a bedroom", "I'll be 10 minutes" Jenna called back. "Mum said you have to come now because we need to get the boxes unloaded" argued Jake. "But I...." Jenna went to argue back but it was too late Ed had disappeared back into the house. Tutting loudly and mumbling to herself she climbed back through the now wedged gate and jogged up the steps that led to a patio and into the house through the French doors where Ed had gone.

The kitchen was huge! Even with boxes and bags everywhere the space compared with the old house was amazing, her Dad was kneeling on the floor in front of a huge cream coloured range cooker that he was attempting to light. The house felt so cold, Jenna guessed he was trying to get some heat going by lighting the old-fashioned oven. Her grandmother had had one just the same and once lit she knew it would warm the whole house in no time. Finding her way through the hallway she came to the foot of the long wooden stair case. Hearing her mothers voice Jenna ran upstairs to be with her. As she got to the top of the stairs she spotted her mum standing by the window in the first bedroom, her hands on her hips. "You OK Mum?" Jenna asked gently. Her Mother jumped slightly but turned around with a bright smile and nodded towards the window, Jenna walked over to see what her Mum was looking at. As she approached the window it all became clear, the view from the window was breath-taking, it felt like you could see for miles. The Autumn sun had come out and touched all the trees in the woodland beyond the paddock making them look as if they were on fire. Jenna could only utter one word "WOW", her mum wrapped a loving arm around her waist and pulled her close. "I think we are going to be quite happy here" she whispered.

4

---

*H*aving bagged the bedroom at the back of the house with the view across the paddock and woods Jenna had been busy unpacking her boxes. The removals men had arrived shortly after the family and had kindly put her bed back together along with more boxes than Jenna could remember packing. The room had white washed walls and bare floorboards which felt strangely warm under foot. It was starting to get dark out side and with the view no longer distracting her Jenna started to make progress on the never ending heap of boxes. Jenna was looking for a specific box which she had marked with the word FRAGILE in big bright red letters. Ripping off what seemed like miles of sticky tape she finally sprung open the box the reveal a sea of bubble wrap, inside each cocoon of packaging she took care to reveal, were her precious horse figures. Smiling she placed each one carefully on the windowsill, taking care to position them just right. Despite the lack of curtains and carpet Jenna sighed satisfied, now it felt like home!

Her mum appeared at the door dragging some enormous black sacks which contained pillows and a duvet and she stayed to help Jenna fit clean white covers on to them. Dinner time soon approached and her parents had mentioned that they were all going to check out the local pub which was a five-minute drive from the farm and sounded like the perfect end to a busy but exciting day for them all.

On the way to the pub Jenna daydreamed of what she might find tomorrow when she went exploring beyond the paddock, she couldn't wait to see what hidden treasures she might find from old barns to tumbling streams in the woods. As her dad turned the car into the car park of the small thatch-roofed pub the headlights illuminated its name painted in large black letters across the side of the building, The Red Fox. Cool name thought Jenna and once they had parked they all headed into the warm bar which was filled with delicious smells and a roaring fire.

Whilst they waited for their food to arrive Jenna and her dad studied the pictures and posters on the cluttered walls. Jenna was immediately drawn to a large black and white photo which she had already spotted depicted a number of smartly turned out horses being paraded past some old cottages. "Hey Dad look at this one" she called. Her dad Martin looked closer at the photo and laughed,"Trust you to find one with horses on" he chuckled. "It has a caption at the bottom he said but it's pretty faint" he continued. Jenna leaned in for a closer look and sure enough she could make out the words 'July 1934 - Brannton horse fair'. Brannton was the name of the village they had moved to! "Oh wow Dad , they have horse fairs here" grinned Jenna excitedly. "They DID" laughed her dad, "Not sure if they are still going now" he continued. "They sure do" came a voice from behind them, a tall lady with curly blonde hair had arrived with plates of steaming food, her kind looking face made Jenna instantly like her and made her brave enough to ask more about the horse fair.

The lady's name was Victoria and she was the owner of the 'The Red Fox', and as it turned out a horse lover like Jenna. After delivering the food she left the family to enjoy their meal but promised to return after to tell them about the area and of course answer Jenna's questions about the horse fair. Whilst they hungrily ate their food, Jenna's eyes scanned the rest of the pub walls for anything else horse related and was not disappointed as her eyes were drawn to horse bits of all shapes and sizes and a huge cart horse collar hung over the stone fireplace.

Sure enough after the family had finished their meals Victoria re appeared to take the empty plates away but came straight back and started chatting away about Brannton village and how she had lived there all her life. 'The Red Fox' it turned out, had been passed down through Victoria's family and had strong links to the Horse fair which had once upon a time been held within its grounds when it had first been started. The Horse Fair was held twice a year just one mile up the road, on the outskirts of the village, at a place called 'Heytons Holding' .

"Which months are the fairs held in?" asked Jenna excitedly " July and October usually" replied Victoria "The next one is in 2 weeks' time!" she continued. Jenna felt herself catch her breath, this was just what she had wanted to hear! " Don't get any ideas" laughed her dad. "We've only just arrived here without you dragging us off to the nearest horse event you can find!" Jenna folded her arms and pouted her lips at him, "That's so unfair" she whined. "She could always come with me" suggested Victoria who had given Jenna a quick wink and smile. Martin raised his eyes and her mum just laughed but they both nodded, "Yessss" squealed Jenna "Thank you Victoria, I would love to" she could have hugged Victoria but resisted. The next two weeks were going to drag!

5

___

*O*pening one heavy, sleep laden eye, Jenna stirred from her dreams. Was she still dreaming? Or was it all true about moving to a farm in the countryside? She opened her other eye and sat up. The gap in her curtains revealed that it was in fact all true! There beyond the windowsill was the paddock and the wood just as she remembered.

Throwing her covers back she swung her legs out of bed and hurried to get dressed. She couldn't wait to explore the farm and discover it's secrets, what would she find?

As she dragged her curtains wide and peered out across the heavenly view, her eyes searched the paddock and followed the line of the woods taking in all the Autumn colours of the trees. It was so beautiful, the paddocks grass sparkled with dew as if it were sprinkled with diamonds. As she was about to turn away something caught her eye over in the bottom corner of the paddock where it joined the woods.

The shape and size made it look like the top of a building but a thick coating of Ivy cleverly covered and hid it's true identity. That was it, Jenna could look no longer, she spun round and headed for the stairs. As she reached the kitchen her mother stood cooking breakfast, her mum opened her mouth to greet Jenna and ask if she wanted some Jenna just yelled " Exploring!" and ran out the door pulling her boots on as she went.

The fresh autumn air made her shudder but she didn't slow her pace, she pushed open the gate and jogged across the glistening grass leaving footprints as she went. As she crossed the top of the hill she could see that what she had spotted in her bedroom was a building,- not just a building it was a series of small buildings, was it what she thought it was? Running down the hill her heart beat so hard she thought it would explode but she carried on, as she got to the buildings she couldn't believe her eyes.

"Stables" Jenna shouted the words just so she believed them! " We've got stables!" she whispered to herself.

The stone built buildings consisted of two blocks of two stables and a small barn which only had part of it's roof still there, The stables all looked usable except for one who's door hung half off . Thick ivy and brambles wrapped themselves round the main walls and rooves, making them look forgotten and ramshackle. Under Jenna's feet a cobbled courtyard revealed itself although with its moss covering it looked like part of the paddock.

A sudden noise in the woods made Jenna jump. As she spun around she spotted a roe deer looking back at her, the animal hesitated for a second before spinning on its heels and dancing off through the trees and out of sight. "Wow" Jenna whispered, this place was like magic. She was desperate to explore the woods but a familiar rumbling in her stomach told her she needed breakfast first. Fuelled with excitement she jogged back to the house stopping half way to turn round just for a last quick look at the stables, she made a quick "eeeekk!" noise and raced to the kitchen. Her mum was still cooking bacon and eggs and was giggling to herself as Jenna burst in. "Happy?" she laughed. Jenna wrapped her arms around her waist and buried her face in her long hair " Thank you" she whispered. "Don't thank me, thank your dad's new job" her Mum replied.

ith the Village shops just a short walk away from the farm Jenna had already planned a shopping trip with some of her birthday money. She had spent the whole evening writing lists and drawing up plans for repairing the stables and barn. The lists were long! Her dad had gently knocked at her bedroom door and sat next to her on the bed laughing and shaking his head at the pages of lists and the pile of ripped up sketches that had formed a small mountain by the bed. "Jenna" he said still laughing "will you slow up a bit? "We've only been here a few days and you already have a livery yard planned!" "Oh wow a livery yard!" Jenna gasped, "Amazing idea Dad well done" and she immediately started writing down a list of yard names.

"Jenna, stop!" her dad gasped. He put his hand on top of the paper and looked her in the eye. "I know you are excited about the whole moving house, and the land and buildings but we need to plan things properly" he smiled. Jenna sat back and folded her arms. " I know what I'm doing Dad" she scowled " This is like all my dreams coming true, if I get the stables fixed I could buy my own horse!" Her eyes welled up and she wiped them quickly with the grubby sleeve of her shirt. "Jenna, getting your own horse is a long way off love" her dad said gently. "We've never had to look after a horse before and as far as I'm aware it's not like having a dog!" Wrapping a strong arm around her shoulders he pulled her close. "I promise that one day we will get you your own horse but let's just take one step at a time". "So you PROMISE I can have a horse one day?" Jenna sniffed hopefully. Her dad nodded slowly "Tell you what he said, why don't you go to the Red Fox tomorrow and see Victoria ? I'm sure she will know about all the local stables and possibly a tack shop?"

Jenna's face immediately brightened and she smiled a little. It was a good plan, giving her Dad a huge hug she flew up the stairs. Jumping onto her bed she kicked her legs with excitement and lay back on the soft pillows, there was something missing though. Someone her age to share the excitement with, she needed to get out and find some friends. She wasn't starting her new school for a couple of weeks but felt she needed a friend before then. Perhaps Victoria at the Red Fox pub could help with that too? She was desperate to tell someone about what had happened with the grey horse and needed reassurance that she had done the right thing by cutting it free as she couldn't understand why the scruffy man had been so angry when all she had done was try and help. Jenna was still worried about what had happened to the horse after they had driven away. Perhaps one of the locals would know the owner of the farm? She would ask Victoria about that too. She couldn't just forget about the beautiful grey gelding and she had to know what had happened to him.

7

*A*fter eating a steaming bowl of homemade vegetable soup and a pile of crusty bread and after digging out her favourite pale blue hooded top which still smelt of the old house, Jenna grabbed Betsy's lead and clipped it onto the small scruffy dog. She would need some company whilst walking to The Red Fox to see Victoria and ask about local riding stables and if there were any kids her age living close by. Walking along the rough edged road she became aware of how quiet the countryside was, stopping to lean on a wooden gate she shut her eyes and listened to the noises around her. The first thing she noticed was the bird song and how clear it was. Jenna could clearly make out at least four different birds singing not that she knew which birds made which noise. As she opened her eyes again she scanned the field and its occupants which happened to be a group of shaggy sheep.

Jenna loved all animals and sheep were such odd creatures with their thick wool and cloven feet. Just as she was about to turn she noticed one sheep lying on its own by the fence. Something didn't look right so tying Betsy's lead to the gate she climbed over. As she approached the sheep as it tried to jump up but immediately Jenna noticed its foot was caught between two strands of wire, falling onto its side the poor sheep let out a sore throated cry. "OK, OK" she whispered to it as she crept nearer and knelt down by its side. Reaching out her hand, she grabbed its leg but was immediately knocked flat as the sheep made another break for freedom. "Ouch!" Jenna's face felt sore and hot, then she realized that the sheep had struck her with its free back leg. "I'm trying to help you so hold still" she told it crossly. Standing up so she was out of harm's way she reached down and with all her strength pulled the two strands of wire apart just enough for the sheep to wriggle free. It leapt to its feet and limped off a short distance before stopping briefly to bleat angrily in her direction, "You're welcome" she laughed and headed back to the gate. Betsy was very pleased to see her and leapt up and down until Jenna grabbed her up into her arms. The little dog trembled and Jenna guessed that the poor thing had probably never seen a sheep before!

Heading back off down the road toward the village Jenna quickened her pace, she had so many questions to ask Victoria and she needed to know where she could get her horsey "fix". She loved all animals, big and small, and her dream had always been to have her own farm where she could rescue sick and unloved animals and nurse them back to health. Even as a small child she had built many snail farms and had even painted white numbers on some of the poor creatures shells so she could tell them apart and plot where they had slid off to! Betsy had been the families only pet and the little dog had such a funny little character that the whole family adored her. She had come from a local rescue centre as a puppy after being found in a box left on the church steps along with four of her brothers and sisters. Jenna could never understand why people couldn't respect animals and her need to help every living creature had grown from there.

8

*R*eaching the door of The Red Fox, Jenna could hear the sound of people chatting and laughing and it immediately put her at ease. She had been getting more and more nervous about walking into a strange place with unfamiliar people but as she had got nearer to the pub the burning questions in her head kept her marching on. Pushing open the heavy glass fronted door she was immediately met with a rush of warm air, her eyes quickly scanned the bar and she spotted Victoria standing behind it serving drinks. Before Jenna could take another step forward Victoria looked up and spotted her and called out, "Jenna! How are you? Come on in Sweetheart". Breathing a sigh of relief Jenna's face lit up in a huge smile and she joined Victoria by the bar. "Give me two minutes and I will be on my break" smiled Victoria, "go grab that table over there and I will bring you over a lemonade" she continued. Soon enough they were both sitting chatting away like old friends and of course Jenna had bombarded Victoria with a million horse related questions and had soon learnt that there was indeed a tack/feed store just beyond the village called Hanson's Country Store and that it stocked everything from pony nuts to riding hats.

Jenna had excitedly told Victoria about the farm her discovery of the stables and barn by the woods and her plans to fix them up somehow. Victoria had laughed at the thought of such a young girl with such huge plans but she admired her spirit. Whilst they were chatting Jenna had mentioned about the grey horse she had seen on the run down farm and what had unfolded that day. As Victoria listened her face slowly saddened, she knew exactly where Jenna was talking about. "That's the Madden's place" she said quietly "They are a strange family who have lived in Brannton for decades", "they have a history of not looking after their animals well and they are not the most popular residents shall we say" she continued. Jenna swallowed hard "Why do they have animals if they cant look after them?" she asked softly. "We don't know to be honest" replied

Victoria "Probably because they have always kept animals. They go off to farm sales and auctions every so often and always seem to bring something else back". "Not for long though" a gruff voice from behind them made Jenna jump a little and as she turned to look an old gentleman in grey tweed approached their table. "Hi George" said Victoria her face lighting up. "Have you got some gossip for us?" she asked him. "Well yes I do actually" George laughed "When I went past the Maddens place 2 days ago there was a for sale board outside, looks like they are finally moving".

"Well I never" Victoria replied. " I thought they would never leave that farm, their family have been there for so long" she continued. "What will happen to all the animals?" asked Jenna quickly, her immediate thought was of the beautiful grey horse she had seen there. "I have the gossip on that too" smiled George "That horse is entered for the Brannton auction, the Maddens reckon it's wild and unrideable!" It was Victoria's turn to laugh, shaking her head in disbelief "Those Maddens couldn't train a rocking horse let alone a living, breathing one!" She scoffed. " I bet you there is nothing wrong with it and they don't want to lose face". Jenna's heart by now was beating so fast she was sure that both George and Victoria could hear it. "Do you really think they will take it to the auction?" she asked quickly. Victoria turned to face her with a glint in her eye. "Well we will soon know in a few days" she winked.

*J*enna had literally run the whole way back to 'High forest Farm', both she and Betsy had arrived by bursting through the kitchen door in a panting mess. "what on earth.." started her startled mother. "There's a horse , the grey horse" Jenna spluttered as she gasped for breath. "A horse, where, Jenna? What are you on about, calm down!" her mum urged. "Remember the horse I saw on the way here? Well its going to Brannton auction because the horrible owners are moving" Jenna was talking so fast her mum looked taken aback. "Jenna you only dealt with that horse once and it was clear then that it was half wild! Why are you so taken with it?" she sighed. Jenna slumped into one of the hard wooden kitchen chairs. "There was something special about that horse I just know it" she whispered softly.

Sitting down beside her ,Jenna's mum gently held her hand and smiled. "Are you trying to hint that we go to the auction and buy it?" she laughed. Jenna raised her eyes to meet her mothers, her answer was one word "Yes". "But Jenna we don't have the knowledge to own and care for a horse by ourselves" she sighed. "Its a wonderful idea but you cannot be serious? Think about what you are saying love"we haven't even met the villagers yet or had a proper look around the area" she said firmly. "We've met Victoria!" pleaded Jenna, "I haven't got a single friend my age here and I just want something to focus on" . Jenna;s mum could hear the sadness in her voice and really felt for her daughter but the idea was crazy. With both of them falling silent, Jenna scraped back her chair and plodded out of the kitchen toward to paddock. Watching her go her mum felt a knot in her stomach. She had never known Jenna be so passionate about something and perhaps there could be worse things to be passionate about?

Leaning on the wooden gate with her chin resting on her hands Jenna let a hot tear roll down her cheek. Wiping it quickly away she sniffed any further tears back and sighed, would any one else ever understand how she felt about horses? Perhaps her mum was right and she didn't have enough knowledge to look after her own horse but how was she to learn without being given the chance?

Hearing her dad's voice in the kitchen she decided to go down to the empty stables and explore a bit more she knew her mum would be telling him about her daughters crazy idea. A chilly breeze was drifting across the valley and Jenna wrapped her arms around herself to keep warm, she started a steady jog towards the tatty buildings. She could just imagine what they were going to look like when they were smartened up, with new rooves and fixed doors she was sure they could be an ideal place to keep a few horses let alone one. As she got to the barn she walked around the outside checking out its high walls and brickwork.

As she reached the large wooden double doors, Jenna gently pulled on one of the rusted handles and quite unexpectedly the door creaked open before it dropped slightly and dug into the weedy ground. It didn't matter though as Jenna was able to squeeze through the gap and into the darkness of the barn. Once her eyes had adjusted to the poor light she spotted the shape of a window at the back, she carefully picked her way over the clutter and bricks which lay all over the floor. With a bit of effort she managed to swing the wooden shutter back and pale sunlight poured in turning the dust particles to glitter as it went. An array of old tools and buckets lay heaped in one corner and hanging from the wooden beams in the roof hung an old set of horse harness. "Wow" whispered Jenna to herself as she walked towards it. Although it had a thick layer of dust hiding its true condition and age the brass buckles still glinted in places as it caught the sunlight. Standing on some of the old bricks Jenna managed to lift the harness free from its hooks but the vast weight had caught her off guard and it slumped to the dusty floor closely followed by her.

"What are you doing?" came a familiar voice in the door way. It was her Brother Ed, he had wandered down to the buildings to tell Jenna that dinner was only about half an hour away. Helping her up he laughed at his sisters dust covered clothes, "Need a little help" he laughed as she brushed herself down. "I was just exploring and found this harness" she replied. "I think its really old" she continued. "Well lets drag it outside and take a proper look" he offered and between them they carefully dragged the filthy harness out through the narrow door way.

The Collar of the harness was enormous and Jenna guessed it had fitted a Shire horse, the leather felt so stiff and dry that it was clear it had hung in the barn for a good long time. Ed had disappeared back into the barn and came out with an old plastic bucket. "What are you going to do with that?" Jenna asked him. " Just you wait and see" he winked and jerked his head in the direction of the stables. Pulling some ivy out of the way Ed smiled and with a "Ta dah!" He revealed a large metal tap, after a bit of effort he managed to turn the tap and release a spluttering flow of crystal clear water which he filled the old bucket with. Diving back into the barn Ed reappeared with some old rags and with Jenna's help they started to wash the dust from the harness. "Thank you" smiled Jenna, it wasn't often her brother spent time doing anything that interested her but she was grateful for his company in this new place.

10

When Jenna woke up on the Friday morning before the auction she felt an uncomfortable knot in her stomach. She was excited about going to her first horse auction but a nervous fear spread through her body when she remembered the beautiful grey horse. Who would buy him and what would happen to him? She had read about so many horses being rescued from auctions in terrible condition or being shipped off to make pet food in huge noisy lorries. Trying to swallow down the lump that had appeared in her throat she pulled her covers up tight to her face. She knew she had only seen the grey horse once and how could anyone be so captivated by an animal they had only met for a few minutes? But there was something about that horse that she couldn't get out of her mind.

The noise of car tyres crunching on the gravel of the drive and the sound of a familiar voice greeting her mum made her scramble quickly out of bed and throw on some leggings, a baggy sweater and race down the stairs. In the kitchen sipping from a mug of tea stood Victoria, with her looking shy and awkward stood a young girl with a pale, freckle covered face which was half covered by a mop of curly brown hair. " Ah Jenna, perfect timing!" her mum smiled, "Victoria's bought someone to meet you". " Morning love" grinned Victoria " this is Zoe and I think you two might just become friends seeing as you both are as animal mad as each other" she winked.

Jenna feeling a little awkward blushed but took a deep breath and asked Zoe the ultimate friend question, "Do you ride?" As a relieved smile spread across Zoe's face she flicked her long hair over her shoulder "Of course I ride, I've got my own pony called 'Flame'" she beamed. That was it, a friendship was born and after Jenna had scoffed down a bowl of cereal they went to explore the paddock and stables which Jenna had been so excited to share with someone. Victoria had gone a long for a quick look too and made Jenna's day when she said that she thought the stables would only take a little work to get them horse friendly. Before leaving the girls to explore on their own Victoria had arranged with Jenna that she would call at 9am to collect her ready to go to the auction. The actual selling of the horses didn't start until 10.30am but Victoria had explained that along side the horses people brought along everything from old tack to chickens and ducks.

Jenna's mind had whirled at the thought of it all and she knew her parents were keen to get some chickens so that the family could have fresh eggs, perhaps she could get some tomorrow?

"This place is pretty cool" grinned Zoe as she crept into the old barn, "I bet there are some really old things in here". Remembering the harness she and Ed had dragged out and washed Jenna excitedly told Zoe about her plans to get her own horse and was keen to ask Zoe about her own pony Flame. It turned out that Flame had been bought out of Brannton auction as a yearling and had been far from tame when he had arrived to be sold. Zoe explained how her mother had fallen in love with the skinny, long legged baby who's mane had been the colour of a glowing fire and although he had crashed around the auction pens, she knew he would soon become friendly and trusting with a bit of time and patience. They had paid only £100 for him and had named him Flame after his beautiful mane, Jenna was desperate to meet Flame after hearing all about him and hoped that after tomorrow's auction they might have time to.

Zoe had been invited to stay for dinner which she had excitedly accepted and after a quick phone call to her parents to confirm it the girls had raced up to Jenna's bedroom to chat more about life in Brannton and of course tomorrows auction. The knot in Jenna's stomach was still firmly there as she told Zoe about the grey horse at the Madden's farm and how even though she had only had a brief sighting of it she just knew there was something special about it. Zoe's eyes had lit up and she laughed as Jenna recalled how Victoria had said that the Madden's couldn't ride a rocking horse!

Both girls fell back on the bed laughing as Zoe mentioned how her dad had once called to the farm to buy some chickens from the Maddens but the next morning the whole family had been awoken by the sound of cockerels crowing, the Maddens had sold them Cockerels instead of hens! "My dad was soooo mad" she giggled "he hates getting up early at the weekend, but the noisy cockerels had started yelling at 5am, poor dad was in the garden trying to wrestle two angry birds into a cardboard box, the chickens were screeching and mum was yelling" she roared, barely able to breathe! " Did he take them back to the Madden's place" laughed Jenna holding her stomach. "Oh yeah" Zoe continued "He went down there in his pyjamas!" Both girls were making such a noise that Jenna's mum came upstairs to check on them.

After a huge dinner Jenna's mum had driven both girls back to Zoe's house to drop Zoe home. The girls had hugged each other like they had been friends for years and Jenna's relief at finding a perfect horsey friend in the same village was written all over her face.

11

---

*W*aking up at 8am on Saturday morning Jenna opened a single, heavy, sleepy eye and turned to fumble her alarm clock silent. Today was the day of the auction and although she was excited to be going with Victoria and her new friend Zoe the knot of nervousness still sat firmly in her stomach. "Just chill out will you?" she whispered to herself as she sat up and swung her legs over the side of the bed. Did she really need to be up this early? She had a clear hour before Victoria arrived to pick her up but she had been so scared of over sleeping that she was not taking any chances.

Plodding over to her wardrobe she pulled the creaking door open carefully so not to wake the rest of the house. Pulling out a pair of blue denim jeans, a longsleeved cream top and a red checked shirt that she had put ready last night before bed she hung them on the radiator and headed for the bathroom. The bright light made her blink as she turned it on but she quickly washed her face and dried it with a fluffy towel before skipping back to her bedroom to pull on her now warm clothes. Teaming her look up with a pair of thick grey boot socks, she crept down the creaking stairs keeping to the edges of the steps to lessen the noise. It turned out she wasn't the only one up as in the kitchen sitting at the breakfast bar was Ed. "Morning squirt" he muttered through a mouthful of cornflakes. "Why are you up so early?" Asked Jenna slightly confused that her usually lazy brother was up and dressed before 11am on a Saturday. "I'm coming with you" he grinned "sounds like it could be an interesting day and there's not much else to do round here Plus Mum said she wants a couple of chickens, so I'm on a poultry hunting mission" he beamed. Jenna although surprised by her brothers enthusiasm, was secretly glad he was coming along as it meant that if her parents were looking to get some animals for the farm already she might be one step closer to maybe getting her own horse one day?

After stuffing down her breakfast and brushing

her teeth and hair in record time, Jenna sat at the breakfast bar nervously drumming her fingers on the polished wood as she waited for Victoria to arrive. Her mind was full of both excitement and anxiety for what the day would bring, as her mind drifted off on its own the sound of a car horn bought her back to reality. She half leapt and half fell from the stool she had been sitting on as she raced for the door. "Come on Ed" she yelled as she bundled her thickest coat on and jogged out to awaiting car.

Zoe was sitting grinning and waving away in the front seat and as Jenna dived in the back seat she was closely followed by Ed who had dressed more like he was going to a house party than a horse sale!

It only took them about ten minutes to get to the other side of Brannton and as Jenna had expected there were a fair few horse trailers and lorries heading the same way. Victoria had chatted about what to expect and had warned not to touch any horses without her being there as some were not as friendly as they first looked and could lash out if spooked. Jenna promised she would stick to her like glue and Ed just nodded and said he wasn't interested in the horses just the chickens. The girls all giggled and Ed blushed slightly and shifted in his seat, he was starting to sound like a country boy after all. "We're here" smiled Zoe as she turned to grin at Jenna who was nervously playing with her wayward hair.

Victoria guided the car into a parking space in the makeshift car park which consisted of a field marked off with bright blue rope held up by skinny metal posts. Jenna immediately started scanning the trailers and lorries for any sign of the grey horse and its cruel owners but amongst the sea of prancing ponies and hairy cobs being trotted around she could see no sign. "Come on guys let's get indoors it looks like its going to pour down in a second" winked Victoria as she caught Jenna's eye, she knew how strongly Jenna felt about the grey horse and it reminded her of herself growing up and wanting something so badly it hurt.

The actual sale ring was inside a huge cattle barn and consisted of tall metal gates coupled together in a circle with a corridor of gates leading to more metal pens where horses and ponies of all shapes and sizes were being groomed and moved about. Ed had already shot off in the search of chickens so the three girls headed into the corridors separating the pens from the public. A pretty little chestnut show pony of about 12hh caught Jenna's eye first, it looked so cute with its badly done mane plaits which resembled hairy ,wonky golf balls. Attached to the pen was a laminated sheet of paper which gave the ponies name and age and a brief history of its winnings.

'Golden Piper, 10yo Chestnut gelding, good wiv kids'

Jenna smiled as she read trying not to laugh at the spelling. They had an hour before the sale started and Victoria guided the girls around the sale pens chatting and discussing each and every pony and horse with the girls who lapped up every word. It was clear Victoria knew her stuff when it came to horses and within a second she could scan a horse from ears to hooves picking up every lump and bump or conformation mishap. "Some people bring their old horses here just to get rid of them" she said sadly, "I couldn't never do that to mine" said Zoe " Why can't people keep them and give them a retirement?" she sighed "Not all people are as dedicated as some of us" Victoria smiled. With that a loud crash and a shout of 'Watch your backs' rang out behind them and they all spun round to see what was happening. I group of burly men were stood in the corridor shouting and waving their arms up and down, "What's going on" Jenna quickly asked Victoria "I'm not sure but I reckon they have a loose horse they are trying to pen,come on lets go and see what's happening" Victoria replied. "Stick close to me just in case it gets past the handlers" she continued.

As they started towards the crowd the shouting and arm waving became more frantic and before they could get any closer Victoria yelled at the girls to grab the rails. Doing exactly as they were told the girls grabbed the freezing metal rails of the pens in the nick of time as through the sea of checked shirts trailing a long rope behind it burst a grey horse. Without a second thought Jenna reached out and grabbed the gate of an empty pen next to her and threw it open. "Jenna what are you doing?" shouted Victoria but before Jenna could answer the grey horse darted into the pen sliding on the straw covered concrete as it went. Slamming the gate shut Jenna let out a long breath and immediately noticed her hands were shaking.

"Jeez Jenna, you frightened me to death doing that but well done" Victoria sighed as she put an arm around her shoulder. "Please don't try that again, you were lucky that horse went in there and not over the top of you." Jenna, still shaking had surprised herself with her quick thinking. "That horse is beautiful" whispered Zoe as she approached the gate. "He sure is" replied Jenna "This is the horse I told you about, The one that belongs to the Maddens".

The grey horse was spinning around the pen frightened by the trailing rope that hung from his neck. His long mud encrusted mane flowing in a tangled mess past his neck. "Steady boy, steady" Jenna whispered to him. The horse slowed it's panic and turned to look at her with its deep black eyes but before Jenna could say another word Jack Madden yanked the gate open knocking Jenna backwards. "Hey watch it Jack" said Victoria crossly as she grabbed Jenna's jacket to steady her. "Get out my way then" he replied gruffly, "This stupid horse needs teaching some manners" The grey horse immediately panicked again smashing into the rails at the back of the pen. Jack Madden grabbed the trailing rope and wrapped it round the rails pulling it with all his weight. The grey leapt forward and as it did he tied the rope tightly to the rail causing the horse to rear and thrash as it tried to escape the rope that was now digging tightly into its throat. "You can't leave it like that!" screamed Jenna as Jack Madden slammed the gate shut again. But he just looked her up and down smirked and strode off without a backwards glance. "Victoria what do we do? We can't leave him like that,he can't breathe" begged Jenna, "we need to get that rope off his throat" Zoe continued. "I'm going to find one of the handlers" said Victoria quickly. "Do not go in that pen, do you promise?" . Both girls nodded as she raced off through the pens.

The grey horse was still plunging and its breathing was starting to become hard work. "I can't wait" gasped Jenna and she ran to the gate of the empty pen next door. "Jenna don't go near it, we don't know what it will do" begged Zoe but Jenna couldn't stand by and watch the horse die in front of her. As she approached the rails where the rope was tied she quickly and quietly tried to untie the knot but it had pulled so tight it was impossible. "Come on boy" she whispered slipping her hand through the rails towards the horses flared nostrils "I need you to come this way" she pleaded. The horses eyes had gone bloodshot and beads of sweat ran down his muzzle and dropped onto the floor. "Please, come on, just a little this way" Jenna whispered in desperation. As her fingers reached his nose the horse flinched then relaxed a little stumbling forward towards her. Jenna's heart was beating so fast that she could feel it in her ears. She gently walked her fingers up his face and towards the rope that dug into its neck. "Please don't move" she pleaded as her icecold fingers felt for the release point in the rope. "Steady, steady" she breathed as she stretched every inch of her arm through the rails.

The horse weakening started to lower his head and Jenna managed to slip her fingers under the tight rope and eased it up just enough to quickly pull it clean over the horses sweat soaked ears. Feeling the instant release the horse shot backwards crashing again into the rails behind he then stood and shook himself blowing his nostrils repeatedly. "Jenna, that was amazing but so dangerous" squealed Zoe as she appeared beside her hugging her friend tightly. "I know" said Jenna "but I couldn't just stand there she stuttered, a hot tear running down her face. As she brushed the tear away Victoria appeared at the pen with a younger man carrying a stick. "How did it get loose" she asked the girls with a relieved tone in her voice, but one look at Jenna told her the answer to that question. "Jenna was amazing" " she calmed him down and got the rope off" said Zoe excitedly. "Jenna, I told you not to go in the pen with that horse!" Victoria scolded crossly. "I didn't go in the pen,I leant through the rails" replied Jenna with a nervous smirk. Victoria shook her head and although she was cross with Jenna she respected the courage the girl had shown. "Please don't try that again" she begged as she joined the girls by the rails" we've only been here half an hour and you've already given me two heart attacks!" Jenna nodded her heart rate slowly returning to normal.

he grey gelding had started to calm down slightly so Victoria suggested that they all went outside to the catering van for a hot drink. As they stood sipping steaming hot chocolate from plastic cups they were joined by Ed who brandishing a plastic crate containing something feathery, excitedly told them how he had got three chickens for £20. Victoria was quick to point out though that what he had bought were in fact some rather angry looking cockerels and that they wouldn't produce many eggs! Both Zoe and Jenna had dissolved into fits of giggles as Ed stomped off back in the direction of the seller who had clearly spotted a 'townie' when he saw one.

"I must admit that grey horse is stunning despite the mess he's in" Victoria sighed. "I'm not sure if anyone would ever get him to trust a human again though" she said glumly. " I would get him to trust again" Jenna replied quietly. "He trusted me enough to get the rope off his throat". Victoria looked deep into Jenna's eyes and saw a piece of herself in them. The sound of a bell being rung broke her thoughts and throwing her now empty cup into the bin behind her she gathered the girls up. "It's sale time!" She told them and with a quickened step they marched back into the barn towards the sale ring and found a suitable place to sit on the huge straw bales surrounding it. Within minutes the straw bales were completely covered with people of all ages most of whom seemed to know Victoria and while she chatted to some of them the girls intently read the sale catalogue that she had given them.

There were a total of 83 horses and ponies entered in the sale although some had clearly been sold outside previous to the sale starting. Jenna knew exactly what she wanted to look up and quickly fumbled through the curled pages to find the grey geldings details.

Lot 41: Grey Connemara gelding
Passported 2011

"SNOW PRINCE"
Vendor: J Madden Esq.

"What a beautiful name" Zoe whispered before Jenna could say the exact same thing. His name made him sound like something out of a fairy tale, although what the horse had been through was like more of a nightmare. As the auctioneer took his stand and read out the rules of the auction the crowd began to hush. "OK folks it's a mighty cold day here today so let's get underway smartish and get these horses sold." With that the gate to the corridor opened and a small bay Shetland mare led by a rather rounded looking man trotted smartly into the ring and the crowd gave an appreciative "ahh". The girls had a ball guessing what would next appear in the ring and what price it would make although Jenna's mind was secretly wishing they would get to Lot 41 sooner rather than later as she literally had no nails left after picking at them since they had sat down.

As quite a few of the horses had been sold outside the ring or withdrawn for sale it didn't take long for the lot numbers to pass through. Beyond the sale ring a familiar shouting could be heard as the grey gelding made his way towards the ring.

Jenna's heart was by now pounding so loud in her chest that she was sure everyone else could hear it, taking some deep breaths she felt a warm arm around her shoulders. Victoria pulled her close and gave her a reassuring wink before letting her go again "It will be alright" she smiled "I'm sure he will find a good home", Jenna wished she felt so confident.

As Lot 40 , a black scruffy cob trotted round the ring Jenna caught a glimpse of Snow Prince heading down the corridor towards the crowd. His nostrils were flared as his lowered head sniffed nervously at the concrete floor as he was ushered along. One of the handlers bringing him up to the sale ring tapped him on his flank with a makeshift flag consisting of a piece of rag tied to the end of a wooden stick. This made the gelding shoot forward and then skid on the hard surface making him panic even more. "Why are they chasing him like that?" Jenna hissed at Victoria. " That's how they move the unhandled ponies around the pens" replied Victoria "It's not easy to get an animal that size to move without a bit of persuasion, especially when its spooking like that".

The sound of the hammer finalising the sale of Lot 40 made Jenna jump slightly and she knew it was time for Snow Prince to enter the ring. As the gate swung open there was an eerie pause and then at last he sprang into the ring shaking his head and swishing his tail as he went. He then stood stock still and sniffed the air, he looked incredible and by the babble of excited chatting that went through the crowd they clearly thought the same. Tapping his microphone the Auctioneer cleared his throat and to read the horse details, "OK folks we've got a smart one here haven't we? A five year old gelding of around 14hh, nice sort but needs more handling" he called out to the crowd. "So where shall we start? £500 I think that's a good start. Come on folks he must be worth that" With that the handler with the flag re appeared and began to chase the gelding round the arena making him snort loudly and prance around the ring with his tail raised and his hooves pointed. "There we go folks look at him now, he would look great with a rider with a bit of work some one start me off at £300" the Auctioneer sang but still not one bid. As the horse floated past them Jenna could feel hot tears well up in her eyes but she held them back, he was so beautiful but there was nothing she could do. Burying her head in her freezing hands she breathed deeply. "OK we've got an offer of £100 so

I'm starting with that" called the Auctioneer "This horse is here to sell to every bid so come guys get yourself a bargain today. One ten, one twenty, one thirty......" The bidding started to increase slowly and then a suddenly leap to £300 made Jenna raise her head and look around the ring to see who was bidding. A tall man lent on the rails was holding three fingers up to the auctioneer, the bidding was hanging on this man's offer and Jenna felt a glimmer of hope as this man had a kindly look about him. "Zoe do you know who that man is bidding?" she whispered to her friend, the look on Zoe's face kind of said it all before she could even reply. "Is he a meat man?" Jenna asked grabbing Zoe's arm. Zoe nodded slowly and held her friend close as she hid her head in her hands once again. Jenna covered her ears this time as she just wanted to block everything out as she couldn't bare to watch him slip away to the meat man.

A sudden shake from Zoe made her lift her head slightly "I cant watch, I just cant" she pleaded but Zoe had the biggest grin on her face that made her ask "What's happened? Why are you grinning?" Zoe simply nodded in Victoria's direction and started laughing. Spinning round to meet Victoria's equally beaming smile Jenna spotted that held in her hands was a bidding card. "What's going on? What happened to Snow Prince?" she pleaded. "He's coming home with us is what's happening" laughed Victoria seeing the confusion and then relief flood into Jenna's pale face. "You mean you bought him?" she spluttered. Grinning and nodding Victoria explained what had just happened, "Your dad rang me last night to talk about the horse and asked me my opinion on him He said he had never seen you so passionate about something and wanted to know if the horse was worth the gamble" she continued., "I said that in my opinion the horse did require a lot of work but that I also felt you had such a passion for this horse that you could give it a good go." Jenna felt huge hot tears fill up her eyes and run down her cheeks, "Really?" she gasped "You're not pulling my leg?" Victoria laughed again "I promise you I'm telling the truth sweetie," "Snow Prince is yours!"

Before Jenna could take everything in Victoria grabbed her hand and led her from the sale ring. "Come on" she said "Let's go find this horse of yours." Linking arms with Zoe, Jenna wiped away the stray tears and tried to make sense of it all, pushing away the confusion she focused on finding where Snow Prince was. It didn't take them long to locate him in one of the loading pens and as they drew closer to the rails he span round to look at them. "Hello boy" Jenna whispered "you're my boy now!" she beamed still half thinking this was all a dream.

"Your parents didn't want you to know anything in case they got your hopes up and we didn't get him" Victoria explained. "You girls stay here, I'm just off to let them know we got him and arrange for someone to take him home for us." The girls nodded silently and then as soon as Victoria left they grabbed each other and lept up and down "Yes, yes, yes!" squealed Jenna her excitement no longer contained. " It's like a fairy tale" smiled Zoe, "I'm sure you will gain his trust soon and Victoria will help you, I know she will" she continued. Snow Prince stood at the back of the pen, resting a hind leg his eyes fixed on the girls."Turn your back on him" whispered Zoe and they both carefully turned around resting their backs on the cold rails. "Why are we doing this?" Jenna whispered back. "You will see" winked Zoe. Jenna was totally confused as to what they were trying to achieve but before she could ask she felt a warm breath on her hair. The gelding had stepped forwards a little and with an outstretched neck was gently smelling her hair. "You must use apple flavour shampoo" giggled Zoe , all Jenna could do was smile as she didn't want to spook him. Snow Prince finished sniffing Jenna's hair and then slowly made his way down her jacket and settled at her pocket which he nudged gently. "I've got mints in my pocket" Jenna whispered. "Give him one" Zoe suggested and ever so slowly Jenna moved her frozen fingers into her left pocket and eased out the packet of mints she had forgotten was there.

As she unwrapped the packet Snow Prince gave her a stronger nudge and she slowly turned around with a flat hand gently offering him a mint. The horse inhaled deeply and with his top lip outstretched he flicked the mint in to his mouth and shot to the back of the pen to eat it. "Good boy" Jenna praised. "Come on, I know you want another" she called holding out another mint on an outstretched hand. " Jenna be careful" Zoe warned. "We don't know what he might do as he's really scared." "I will be careful, I promised" breathed Jenna, holding herself so still despite shivering from the cold. Taking a step forward Snow Prince looked unsure of his next move and paused. Clicking her tongue Jenna encouraged him forward and again he scooped the mint off her hand and stood back again against the safety of the back rails. "What a clever boy" she praised feeling an even greater love for the horse. "Come on let's go and find Victoria and see what's happening" urged Zoe who had turned a funny shade of blue from the cold air! Although she didn't want to leave the horse Jenna now felt a sense of huge relief and an over-whelming feeling of hunger and as they spotted Victoria talking on the phone outside they went out to join her.

13

*A*s the girls got closer to Victoria they could see her excitedly talking to who ever was on the end of the phone and as they got to her she finished the conversation. "Great news girls" she beamed "Zoe's parents Brian and Claire are on their way with their pony trailer to collect Snow Prince and your dad has contacted the auctioneers and has paid for him over the phone" she continued hugging Jenna."So all we need to do is collect his paperwork and he is officially ours!" Both girls high-fived each other and for Jenna it still hadn't sunk in that she now owned a real-life horse!

A sudden thought popped into Jenna's mind, "I haven't got anything for him" she blurted out. "No head collar or buckets or brushes or anything. What about feed and hay?" The panic in her voice was plain to hear but Victoria again just smiled and said "Well we best go and get some then" she winked steering the girls towards the top of the field where the tack stalls and second hand sale was going on.

On the way they caught sight of Ed who was seemed to be in deep negotiations with a seller over a chicken house. Jenna jogged over to him as he shook the other man's hand and the deal on the chicken house was done! "Did you know?" she smiled trying to contain her excitement, "know about what?" Ed grinned back trying to look serious. "You did know!?" "How could you not let on!?" Jenna squealed hitting him playfully in the arm, "I couldn't tell you could I ?" he smiled "What if we hadn't have got him?" "It was better that you knew nothing otherwise you would have been in a total state!" Jenna glared back at him with her hands on her hips "As if I would do that" she scowled As they all headed in to the hustle and bustle of the busy stalls, the girls chatted endlessly about what colour buckets and head collars to get and Jenna fell in love with a powder blue grooming kit in a sturdy box which could also double up as a mounting block. With her birthday money burning a hole in her pocket she started thinking logically about what she might need and asked Victoria for advice. "Just get the basics for now" Victoria suggested, "Buckets, a decent adjustable head collar and some brushes perhaps? The grooming brushes will help you bond with him and he looks like he could do with a make-over" she winked. There was so much to think about that Jenna felt over whelmed, was she really ready for the responsibility of a horse? As her mind whirled with doubts and decisions a friendly arm linked in hers and Zoe appeared at her side, her beaming smile immediately relaxed Jenna "It's going to be OK" winked Zoe, "Come on lets grab what we need and get back to your horse" she grinned and dragged Jenna to a stall selling head collars of every size and colour. A black leather one with glinting brass buckles caught Zoe's eye and although it was the most expensive one there she decided that she wanted Snow Prince to have the best.

Ten minutes later she had arms fully laden with buckets and yard tools and with the last of her money she treated herself to the grooming kit she had seen earlier. Victoria had spotted Zoe's parents arriving with the trailer and they had all gone to greet them. "You must be Jenna?" smiled Claire, Zoe's mum, Jenna nodded shyly and thanked them for coming to collect Snow Prince. "It's no problem at all" continued Claire, "we are so pleased that Zoe has found another horse loving friend to hang out with".

The girls neatly stacked all of the things they had bought into the back of the 4x4 and then everyone headed into the sale barn to get Snow Prince ready for loading. Jenna spotted him quickly and headed for his pen. The beautiful grey stood quietly at the back of the pen, his head hung low. "Is he OK?" Jenna asked Victoria worriedly "He is just tired out" she assured her "He has had a stressful day and needs a good rest, lets get him loaded then he can chill out in the field" she said. "We will have to chase him into the trailer without a head collar on as its been a while since he has had any sort of handling" Victoria explained, "Once he is in the trailer we can try and get the head collar on as he will be contained and might be a bit calmer, horses don't usually forget too much of their basic training but it will take time to build his trust".

With the trailer backed up to the loading ramp and the head collar gripped tightly in her shaking hands, Jenna watched with a thumping heart as Victoria and Brian carefully went into the pen and slowly guided Snow Prince out using their body language. As soon as the horse got into the corridor he shot forward snorting as he sniffed the dirty floor. Clicking her tongue with her arms and hands out stretched Victoria encouraged him the short distance towards the loading ramp. Brian had spread some fresh straw on the lowered ramp and with only the slightest hesitation Snow Prince pranced up into the trailer grabbing a sneaky mouthful of straw as he went!

"Yesss" Jenna breathed as the ramp went up and the top doors closed. Before she could say another word, Brian called to them that he was going to head straight off in case the horse got stressed in the trailer. The girls and Victoria ran to the car park and jumped in the car managing to pull in right behind the trailer as it pulled onto the main road and headed for High Forest Farm.

The journey only took around 10 minutes but Jenna bit her nails all the way. "Just relax love" Victoria reassured, catching Jenna's eye in the rear view mirror. "We are all here to help you I promise, just trust in yourself and then the horse will trust in you". "Horses like to have a leader, they are prey animals and every wild herd has a mare as leader and she is the one that keeps them safe and takes them to fresh grass and water. In a domestic or captive situation you as owner have to act as head mare", Victoria continued to explain. Jenna had read about the exact same thing in one of her hundreds of pony books!

It would take time but she was confident that she could be come not only Snow Prince's leader but his soul mate too.

14

*A*s they followed the trailer into the drive Jenna could hear Snow Prince calling and banging on the floor of the trailer. "He is telling everyone that he's arrived" grinned Zoe and as the car pulled up in front of the house both girls leapt out. Jenna's parents came straight out to meet them and Jenna ran straight to them grabbing them both in a huge hug as she cried tears of relief once again. "Thank you, thank you, thank you" she sobbed into her mum's shoulder, her emotion finally spilling out. "You don't need to thank us", whispered her dad "We uprooted you and dumped you in the countryside so the least we could do was get you something you wanted" he laughed as he scruffed her hair up. "OK Jenna where's that head collar you bought" called Victoria. "Let's get this boy sorted and out in the paddock before he gets upset".

Carefully opening the jockey door on the trailer , Victoria peeped into the darkness and immediately came eye to eye with the gelding. His hot breath blew her hair from her face as he sniffed her face gently. Jenna held her breath as Victoria carefully ran her hand over his soft muzzle and stood up inside the trailer and shut the door behind her.

After a few minutes and a bit of clunking and rocking of the trailer Victoria appeared with a beaming smile on her face. "All done she said winking at Jenna, "He was a little nervous but he soon relaxed and let me pop the head collar straight on, I told you he wouldn't have forgotten much" she smiled. "Right lets get this boy unloaded and into the paddock so he can check out his new home" Victoria suggested. Jenna ran to open the paddock gate and Brian carefully drove into the field and round in a circle stopping just as he came through the gate way again. As he and Victoria undid the top back doors and lowered the ramp everyone waited for Snow Prince to step out into his new home. After a few seconds and a careful turn around in the trailer the gelding took a shaky step down the ramp pausing to sniff it suspiciously and then in a split second he jumped the rest of the ramp cleanly and galloped flat out across the field stopping half way to leap and buck and grab a few mouthfuls of lush green grass. Brian pulled the trailer out of the field and Jenna shut the gate behind him then climbed up to sit on it alongside Zoe to watch Snow Prince dance his way around his new home. With his tail held high and his feet floating over the ground the horse was a vision of beauty as he snorted his nose and shook his mane, obviously pleased to be free from the metal pens that had held him all day.

Brian and Jenna's dad had headed back to the auction to collect Ed and his chickens. Jenna had clean forgotten about her brother in the excitement of getting Snow Prince home and when she mentioned this to Zoe both the girls laughed so much they nearly fell off the gate.

Victoria had gone inside to have a well deserved cup of tea with Jenna's mum, leaving the girls to watch in awe as Snow Prince explored every inch of the field, floating as he went. His paces reminded Jenna of the dressage horses she had watched in videos and visions of her riding into an arena on him swirled in her head. "You need to get some photos of him they day he arrived" suggested Zoe.

"Good plan!" squealed Jenna and she tore into the house and up the stairs to her bedroom to fetch her small digital camera.

After a quick rummage she located it in her bedside table and as she turned to leave she caught sight of Snow Prince prancing around the paddock. The view from her window was like a dream and she did pinch her arm gently just in case it wasn't real before charging down the stairs again and into the paddock to get some photos of Snow Prince as he stood gazing at them from across the paddock.

The sound of a vehicle approaching gave the gelding the excuse to charge around the paddock again and Jenna managed to capture some real action shots of him as he flew past them. The vehicle turned out to be Brian's car and trailer and the girls ran to meet the other new arrivals at High Forest Farm, the chickens! Ed had cleverly shut the chickens in the new house and soon had them unloaded and the run set up on the lawn. He had certainly thought of everything and soon had a feeder and drinker set up ready for the new additions and as he pulled up the hatch on front of the house 3 fat chickens bundled out followed by a large brown egg! The girls dissolved into fits of laughter as Ed joked that at least these ones weren't cockerels!

Jenna still giggling turned to watch Snow Prince again and to her surprise found him leaning over the fence watching the chickens with great interest. "Well it looks like someone has found some new friends" joked Jenna and she slowly walked across to the horse who stood fixated at the new residents. As her hand reached his muzzle he stepped back slightly so she just paused and he carefully stepped forward again sniffing her hand. "Good lad, steady now we can be friends too" Jenna whispered gently to him and as the scruffy grey gently nibbled at her fingers she knew that new adventures awaited the pair of them.

TO BE CONTINUED ...

MYSTERY

Make sure you look out for my next book to discover what Jenna and Snow Prince get up to next.

As Jenna Waters settles into life at High Forest Farm with her family and beloved pony Snow Prince, a new challenge heads their way when a frightened and lost dog needs their help. Where did the dog come from? Who are the men in the white van? Can Jenna and her best friend Zoe solve the mystery and reunite the dog with its rightful owner before the dog thieves strike again? Will Jenna's quick thinking save the day or lead them into more danger?

Thank you for reading!

Sally Marsh x

25787409R00059

Printed in Poland
by Amazon Fulfillment
Poland Sp. z o.o., Wrocław